21

BY VUYO JOBODA

VUYOJOBODA.COM

For permission requests, write to the publisher, addressed "Attention: Permissions Coordinator," 205 N. Michigan Avenue, Suite #810, Chicago, IL 60601. 13th & Joan books may be purchased for educational, business or sales promotional use. For information, please email the Sales Department at sales@13thandjoan.com.

Printed in the U. S. A.
First Printing, August 2021.
Library of Congress Cataloging-in-Publication Data has been applied for.

ISBN 978-1-953156-44-0
www.vuyojoboda.com

Contents

FOREWORD

MY NAME IS VUYO JOBODA. I AM 21 YEARS OLD, BORN AND bred in Cape Town; daughter of Sindiswa and Mzukisi Mndwangu, sister of Ntando and Kwakhanya, and granddaughter of Blossom Joboda. I am a MC, TV presenter, Radio host, Motivational speaker, Entrepreneur, performer, and a film student at the University of Cape Town. I am a dreamer and a visionary with plans and hopes to change the world, particularly eradicating poverty in Africa. This is my first book and I wrote this book to share my heart. In the past 21 years I have gone through some experiences, some that were too much for my age. Through those experiences, I have learned lessons that I will forever cherish. I have decided to share those lessons with you. I am sharing not only my heart but also my pains. I share about rejection, pain, purpose, and some diary moments that I have never shared with anyone before.

I would like to thank everyone who has supported my journey thus far. I would like to thank my mother for being the best friend that I could ever ask for, my dad, my aunt, and her husband for helping me when I needed a hand, and my grandmother for just being there to listen and share valuable lessons filled with wisdom.

This book is a gift to the hustlers, the people who defy the odds and break through barriers placed before them in order to achieve maximum results. The nay-sayers. People so determined to strive that nothing can discourage them.

The book breaks all the conventions of a traditional book. It does not have perfect and precise grammar or diction. It does not have structure. It is just me sharing my heart with you. I hope you will heal, breakthrough, learn and be inspired to be the best version of yourself that you possibly can be by the end of this book.

Lots of Love
Vuyo Joboda

The fires in Joe-Slovo ignited the fire in me!

I was born and raised in the shacks of Joe-Slovo in a township called kwa-Langa a few kilometers away from Cape Town where fires would erupt every month. We slept with our minds and ears alert of the "FIRE, FIRE, FIRE," signal that would be shouted whenever fires erupted. We eventually found ways to save ourselves and the little assets we owned from the deadly fires of Joe-Slovo. This included setting the furniture in a way that will make it easy to remove when a fire erupts.

The number of times fires erupted exceeded my measure of remembrance. There was a time when a fire erupted in the middle of the night, we all woke up and laughed because it was the third occurrence for that month, we laughed because the pain was too much to bear, and the only way we could express the pain was through laughter.

The fires were not even the hardest thing; crime was our daily portion. Every day as I went to school my mother would pray that I come back safely into her arms. The sound of gunshots was my lullaby, and an empty stomach was my bedtime story. Nothing could ever be tantamount to the fear

I experienced as I slept hoping that tomorrow would be a better day.

I would walk 1 kilometer to relieve myself, I would walk another kilometer to get water. I would watch my neighbors greet each other each day with eyes begging for survival, with hearts longing for a slice of bread, for water to drink… for a better life……

In this shack I lived with three strong women, one of these women was the woman who gave birth to me. This woman's strength is stronger than the strongest rock. She gave birth to me when she was young, she had nothing in her name, she had no possession of value, no substance to her existence. She used to say that I was the only valuable thing that she had. She reminded me every day that I was her hope for change.

Those words, uttered when I was five, have stuck with me ever since. From that moment on, I made a choice to be the change! From that moment, I started dreaming. I dreamt, I dreamt, I dreamt. I dreamt of finding hope in my hopeless situation. I didn't know how or why but there was a burning desire inside of me that reminded me that there was hope at the end of my tunnel, hope to fulfill all my ambitions and hope to have a better life. The only thing I could do at that time was dream!

The idea of dreaming was a fantasy, it was unrealistic, it was not in the local vocabulary of my community. In Joe-Slovo there was no hope, the only way to survive was to breathe. Mothers would cry for mercy every night, they would loan sugar and bread just to feed their kids. During all this difficulty, I remembered my dreams for a better life. My dreams for a better life kept on reminding me that this shall not last forever.

My dreaming began to manifest as this burning desire which directed my choices. As that occurred, I was bullied in primary school because I refused to succumb to the standards of what was the norm. I was bullied because I dreamt of change and for a better tomorrow. When my peers would talk about alcohol, boys, or drugs, I would divert conversations to dialogue about creating a prosperous future that would take our families out of poverty and suffering.

For sparking those conversations, I was labeled as weird. I was rejected and laughed at for being the short, lonely girl who everyone thought was weird. No one wanted to talk with me, no one wanted to be friends with me. I used to come home every day and fall into the shoulders of my mother crying.

Every day would be a distinct experience as bullying escalated. It worsened every year because every year my passion for my dream would ignite more fire inside of me.

But through it all I still had the dream in mind and that kept me going. It helped me heal. My dream kept on reminding me that tomorrow will be a better day. I suffered from rejection not only from society but from my father, who left my mother and I a few months after my birth. He did not call on my birthdays, didn't pay child support and he never visited me. I never knew what a father was. For a while I thought I was not meant to be loved, but my mother reminded me that I did not need all that I thought was necessary to travel on the journey to finding my purpose. She said that I had to spend time and energy focusing on the narrow path towards finding and fulfilling the reason for my existence.

It was during these tough times that I got to spend a great deal of time on my own. Rather than hanging out with friends, I would sit alone and write down all my ambitions, hopes and dreams. It was that time where I decided to embrace myself, love myself and appreciate myself. I decided to use that time to work on building my confidence. I spent this time finding out about myself, what I like, what I do not like, my strengths, my weaknesses, my talents, my gifts and everything that makes me who I am.

I became comfortable with the fact that the bullying and suffering was my obstacle that I had to overcome, that I had to break through all the negativity and force the positivity out of those negative situations. Those were some of the best years of my life. Yes, I say they were the best years of my life because it was during that time that I found out that I am talented, smart and even then, had the potential to change my circumstance, change my community and change the world. Those were the best years of my life because they formed me, they groomed me, they strengthened me, they encouraged me, and they motivated me. I discovered *so* much about myself, but most importantly I discovered that I could do anything I put my mind to. The fire that's ignited in me is the fire that makes me understand that I live not only for the sake of being, but that I live for a purpose. I live to make a positive difference in the lives of many through my voice.

Today I am happy, I am stronger, and I am wiser. I am the product of my dreams. I am the product of my mother's prayers. I am a survivor of poverty, rejection, suffering and difficulty. I am currently the first person in my family to study at the University of Cape Town. I am a successful entrepreneur, the owner and founder of Perez Empire, founder of Young Bold and Black, event MC, motivational speaker, TV presenter, radio DJ, performer, filmmaker, *and* an author.

Yes, it took time for my mom to fully support my dreams of being an artist, but she saw my consistency, my passion, determination, hard work and unwillingness to change my mind about my dreams. I am the one who knew what my dream was and therefore I did not allow anyone to deter me from my path. I had to be courageous enough to push through the tough times. We all have that dream that we had as little children. You know this dream, it's inside of you, I do not know what this dream is for you, no one knows what your dream is, you are the only one who knows what the dream is so never allow any circumstance, anyone or anything to take it away.

I stand here today with so much strength and I ask you to be strong in your journey, may your dream give you strength. I could have let my dreams burn in the fires of Joe-Slovo, but I let the fire inspire me, motivate me, and give me hope. Find the hope in your difficulty, find strength in your fires.

TEDx YouthCapeTown 2017— "There is Hope"
—by Vuyo Joboda

CHAPTER 1

BLACK KID INTELLIGENCE

HAVE YOU EVER FELT LIKE YOU WERE BEING CHALLENGED? Not by any particular person or thing, but by life. At this point you should ask yourself if perhaps you or your decisions have put you in the place you are in. A place where you are tired. You are tired of trying because the more you try, the harder it becomes. You feel like you are giving your all in everything you do but still, regardless of all of that, you feel like it's not enough. At this point you do not cry, you do not get disappointed because there is so much disappointment and hurt around you that you have given up being hurt. You feel numb to disappointment and shame. You feel like everything and anything you try fails. However, you have a desire to keep going. You do not know what it is, but you are motivated. That motivation is driven by your memory of where you come from but most importantly the memory of what you dream of, the memory of your hope's, ambitions, and goals. The memory you once had as a child. You did not know that it would be so difficult, you didn't know that there would be times where you are too tired that you are not even sure what to do or where to go. You feel like what you are or who you are is not enough. Some may say the only thing would be to hold on.

When you are looking at the pain, disappointment you are facing, think about the Black kids. Black kids were indoctrinated by colonization by the power of NO. You see the power of colonization was not only in taking material things that we had, but they also took away the understanding of YES. Colonization instilled the idea that we are not good enough, that we are too dark, our hair is too stiff, our voices are loud, our personalities possess too much zest. They made us believe that we should constantly erase the darkness of our skin, strengthen our thick hair, tone down our volume, and reduce our zestful spirits. They invented IQ and made us believe that our intelligence is based on the hegemonies they have created. They made us forget that the intelligence of a black boy and girl is so powerful, it has power in it that it does not see itself higher than anyone else's. The intelligence of a black girl or boy is hard to comprehend, it is the kind of intelligence that can bring upon change to the world. This intelligence has been told NO. The intelligence of a black boy and girl is one that is able to survive in the absence of civilization. The intelligence of black kids is one that enables them to survive poverty. Intelligence of a black child gives him or her the ability to defy adversities. A black child's intelligence is different, it's special. A black child's journey is graced with trials and tribulations, yet still it conquers and strives to seek the motivation to survive. The intelligence of a black child is able to manifest in the absence of Google, it is able to manifest in the absence of tall walls that provide them security. A black child's intelligence is able to manifest in the absence of dinner, in the absence of dessert. The intelligence of a black child manifests in the absence of wool and cotton that guarantees them warmth. The Intelligence of a black child manifests in the absence of a Christmas dinner, in the absence of Happy Birthday. The intelligence of a black child manifests in the absence of a bedtime story, a kiss goodbye, a hug, a "I Love You." A black child is able to manifest their intelligence in the presence of poverty, in the presence of crime, in the presence of hate, in the presence of sewage, in the presence of alcoholic neighbors, in the presence of burning shacks, in the presence of lack of sanitary towels, in the presence of torn clothes, in the presence of absent fathers, in the presence of tired worn-out mothers, in the presence of mothers who are heartbroken by fathers who were once intelligent. A black child has the kind of intelligence that loves and cares. The kind of intelligence that embraces culture, one that is beautiful and different. An intelligence hard to find and difficult to comprehend. This kind of intelligence unites a people in song and dance. It is this intelligence that binds the community in black, it is this intelligence that embraces the absence of an accent that is enforced. It was this intelligence that the colonizers saw, and they said NO. It is this intelligence that intimidated them. It was an intelligence that they had never heard of or seen before. This intelligence that they decided to make inferior. As you are going through your struggle, remember that there is a black girl or boy fighting to prove this intelligence. There is a black girl or boy who has heard, "NO you are not a human worthy of life. You don't deserve to live because you are a black child." If the black child is still able to manifest their intelligence, you too can make it through that challenge. You too have your own struggles. We all have struggles that make us feel inadequate. We are bound to feel that way. You have your purpose, that dream, goal, or vision that you want to achieve. You have been working at it for years, but yet it seems like you are not getting there. There is that one thing that no matter how hard you try, it just never works. You are like a Black child. You work hard at reaching your ambitions but the harder you try, the harder it seems to get. Nothing around you says "yes," you hear "No," you believe the No and the No becomes who you are. You therefore dwell in the No. I am here to let you know that it's okay. It is normal to feel hopeless and helpless, but just like a black child you will look at your obstacles and you will look past them. You will enable yourself to heal, fight and dedicate your time and efforts to making your dreams possible. I wrote this book and I do not know if it is how a book is supposed to be, but I do know that it will help change your life and most importantly change your perspective and remind you how powerful you are.

CHAPTER 2

PURPOSE

Purpose, this by far has been the most beautiful word I have ever seen. Purpose for me has always been a concept that I have been interested in and curious about. According to Google, purpose has two meanings, which both correlate with the other. The first definition of the word is "the reason for which something is done or created or for which something exists." The second definition is "a person's sense of resolve or determination." I think Google nailed these definitions, and I would like to unpack these definitions in detail about what exactly they mean in the context of humanity. I say concept because I believe it is complex, detailed and takes great attention to understand what it is. The concept requires a lot of digging deep, which is not easy.

1. I would first like to unpack the second definition, which is: "A person's sense of resolve or determination."

Two words stand out here namely: Resolve and determination.

Resolve, what is it that you are resolving? There is a problem that needs to be resolved and you are the only person that can resolve it. You are the only person who knows what the problem is and how to go about fixing it. You need to allow yourself to resolve that problem. You are the solution. The world is waiting for you to resolve this problem. We could also look at resolve as the resolve as your solution, what is your resolve to yourself? What are you comfortable with, what makes you click? What can resolve your sense of being? What do you do to resolve all of your problems or even better, feel like you don't have any problems? Think about it, what is your resolve to you? What is your resolve for your soul? What is your sense of resolve? Driven by the power to resolve, what is your sense of determination. What brings out the determined version of you? What brings out the best of you? Determination is simply the willpower to do something. What is it that you are determined to continue doing no matter who says what or what happens?

2. Now, let's go back to the first definition: "The reason for which something is done or created or for which something exists."

Now if we look at this definition it goes to the roots, firstly to the reason why humanity was created. There is a reason why you were born or created and why you exist. Each and everything created is to serve a certain purpose, but the most beautiful creation is the creation of humans. If we take it way back and think about the creation of humanity we will notice that there is so much that happened in Genesis before God created a human. He prepared everything, made sure everything is perfect, well and in order for the human. There was already a value placed on the human because they arrived at a perfect time. So, the first factor to consider is that there was perfection prior to our creation because God had to ensure that all was in order. All things that were necessary for us to strive was made and put in place before we were even created. What fascinates me the most is that no plant in the field had sprung up yet as it had not rained yet, "But there went up a mist from the earth and watered the whole face of the ground," (Genesis 2:6- KJV). This means that nature had to adjust itself and make way for what was yet to come on. Rain was not necessary before this point because there was no reason for it to rain, no reason for the plants to grow as there were no humans to subdue it. But as soon as a human was to be formed, everything aligned with the other to ensure that the human would survive and strive. As soon as everything aligned, humanity was created. This caused a change to everything else which was already in existence. God formed him and breathed into him. Now we often underestimate this "breath." This is not just any breath. God, the creator of everything and anything, breathed *life* into humanity. It was during this time where he transferred the power, the dominion, the strength, the wisdom, and the grace to have rule over the world. The first purpose and only reason why God created all the beauty and abundance of the garden and everything else was so that the humans may work it and keep it. That being the ultimate purpose why the earth was created. Then God gave the human the power to name each and everything which was on the earth. This was another exercise of displaying the power that humanity has on nature. Why am I saying this? Well, I wanted to demonstrate to you that you had purpose even before you were born. The reason you were created was to have dominion. That is the first thing we need to understand about our purpose. You need to understand that everything that is necessary to ensure that you succeed in your purpose is already available, just like the mist made sure that it gathers clouds for rain so that you may eat, also everything is available for your purpose to come alive.

Here are some other reasons why you were created:

a. You were created to add value. Your existence is to add value that will bring about change to what there already is. There is a certain value that you are to add to your family, your community, your country, the world. Your purpose manifesting then is the value. There is no other reason why you were created but to conceptualize, and put in full force, the value that you are to add to humanity. The value that you add is specifically for you, no one can or will add the kind and type of value that you can add to the world because it is generic and specific to you.

b. You were created to dominate. This aspect of the creation is what many people fear, hence they are not able to fully maximize their purpose. It is essential that we realize that each one of us has an innate power that we possess. That power is not drawn from an exterior source, it was breathed to you by God. It is a matter of realizing the power and accessing it in order to allow your value to come out. This form of power is the one that places the responsibility upon you, the responsibility to take domination for your future into your hands. There is no circumstance, no past, absolutely nothing that can limit or deter you from maximizing your purpose, it is a matter of channeling this dominion. There is a distinct value that is in your purpose that no one can take away.

c. You were created to live your purpose. The beauty of it all is that the purpose that God has for your life is so perfect. Imagine living a purposeful life filled with the comprehension of Perfection. Jeremiah 29:11 "For I know the plans I have for you, plans to prosper you and not to harm you, plans to give you hope and a future." God says that He has the best for you, to bring out the best in you because you are the best. By not reaching our full potential with the gifts and talents He has given us is insulting to Him. We are not trusting what He has given us. He has given you that talent, skill, and ability so that He may receive Glory. Whenever I see someone doing something they were born to do, I see the radiance of God, I see His power, I feel His power. I see the manifestation of greatness that is unexplainable and undefinable. My soul gets rejuvenated, healed, and transformed when I see purpose exercised because I think my body, and my being connects to the manifestation of God's original plan during creation. This is a feeling you also feel when you are exercising your purpose. I am not talking about a feeling that you can explain or put words to. This feeling takes you out of you and connects you to your Maker. Whatever it is, you know what it is, and if you have not discovered it, I hope you find it.

Driven by passion, your purpose is what makes you human. It is your contribution that you must give in order for this world to function in full accordance. If everyone would live their purpose, then the world would be a place that correlates and works in accordance, this is because everyone would be playing their part. Many people suppress their purpose because of a fear of rejection and failure. The world will never become a better place if there are still people not fulfilling their purpose. The journey to finding this purpose is unique to every person. No one knows the time and stage at which this is to be realized or understood. The certain truth is that everyone has a set destiny that they should aim for in their time on earth. Everyone has the potential to be great and that greatness can only be tapped into once you live your purpose. Everyone has the potential to be successful if only they tap into their passion that gives them motivation to continue chasing after their dreams and purpose. Some of the most purposeful people are successful because they chose not to hold back and deny their existence, but to fully flesh out their dreams. They did this by taking the necessary steps to take them to their destiny. When they got NO, they went back, improved themselves and tried again. Purpose is the true understanding of who you are, what you love, what you don't love, what makes you happy, and what doesn't. Finding your purpose answers a lot of questions that you might have if you don't find it. Many people live their lives not knowing what exactly it is that they are living for. Being born and being alive is not by coincidence or chance. You are born for a specific reason, a purpose. You are then given an amount of time to find out what that purpose is, live it and overcome every challenge presented by this purpose. Every human being is born distinctively with an identification which is different to another, hence everyone's fingerprint is different. That fingerprint has the writing of your purpose on it. It marks the exclusivity of your purpose and your journey. Your fingerprint identifies you as different to any other human ever to exist on the planet. That alone, should mean great significance to you. This should highlight the power of your individuality. It is something that no one can impart inside you or take away from you as it is engraved in the walls of your heart, in the depths of your soul and in the matter of your brain. What society has embraced in achieving, is covering your purpose with other ideologies they deem to associate with purpose. You find a lot of members of society with their purposes buried underneath what is identified as normality. The first thing would be to remove the ideologies set by society. We are all victims of society's norms and these have a way of deeming our light and our purpose. We need to break through all of that and stand tall in the knowledge of our purposes.

I believe that children portray their purpose at a very young age, however that purpose gets lost in the infiltration of NO's that they receive. Those NO's mute that purpose. The parents are responsible to nurture and embrace that purpose, regardless of the inaccessibility of material things that they mistakenly think is necessary to fulfil that purpose. The first thing would be to realize that purpose. By realize I mean to notice, to see, to be cognizant of what your child's purpose is because every child shows it when they are small. Where do parents assume children get the ability to draw so eloquently at that age? Where do you think the child acquires the ability to hold a note at that age? They have it embedded in their DNA, it is part of them, it is who they are, it is their purpose. Once that pure essence of purpose is lost it is difficult to find it again. At that age it is still raw and uncensored, it is pure and in its original form. Once it is deemed bad by a leather belt imposed by authority, it is very difficult to find it again. Many people then spend years and years trying to figure themselves out, trying to find themselves. I think the question would have to be asked to the parents or guardians, what made you excited about life at the age of 5, what were you able to do without the cognition of an adult?

I believe that we don't need to spend all this time, all these years to find ourselves or discover ourselves because we are already here, we are already beings. We don't have to have life figured out because that is out of our control, but you are in control of yourself. What we need to do is to remove the NO's. We need to remove the fear, the discouragements that have been genetically and culturally embedded in our understanding of humanity. The only true sense of our humanity has been based on the inabilities. There is nothing we can do with how our parents raised us, there is nothing we can do about what our societies told us. What we can do however, is remove the thought of fear, failure, and disadvantage. True beauty of life is in living your purpose. The NO is an obstacle that you have to overcome. An obstacle that many drown in and die in, it kills many souls. Walking around are human beings drowning in NO. They are told that there is a YES, but they are made to believe that they are not worthy of the yes. If only they heard the following words when they drew with crayon on the wall, "Wow my child, this is beautiful. What is this? You are such a great artist, your hands are gifted, you are going to be the greatest artist of all time, you are going to travel the world drawing all possibilities your mind takes you too. Well done my child, continue drawing," or perhaps when he was singing, he was told, "Wow my child, you are so good, your voice is like angels singing, you are going to be the greatest musician of all time. I am so proud of you. What song is your favorite? Here is a remote, pretend it is the mic and I am your audience, perform like you are performing to thousands." Or perhaps when they come back from athletics practice, "My child how was your training session today? Be sure to be better tomorrow. I am proud of you, the more you practice the better you become. Never be discouraged, you are the greatest, you are a gold winner, you are the fastest runner." Or perhaps when he was studying all night, "My child continue to study, you are smart, you are intelligent, you are good, you are an A+ student, you are bright." Or perhaps they could say, "Yes my child, I see that you are talented in this, continue to pursue it, nothing can stop you from achieving and living this purpose. I will support you. I love you." Those words are greater than the plate of food that parents get occupied trying to get, thinking it's all that the child needs. What I am saying is that many parents get trapped trying to provide everything else for the child, but the most important things they need is love, appreciation and support. A child who grows up in the deepest parts of poverty who is fed with words like "you are enough, you are good, you are important, you are smart, you are beautiful, you are capable, you are rich, you are successful, you can achieve anything you wish, the world is your oyster," is much more likely to live a purposeful life than a child dished materialism who is told "shut up, you are annoying, you give me stress, you are such a pain, you are a failure, keep quiet, do as I say or I'll smack you." All a child needs is to be appreciated, that's why God gave the mother milk because it is food that everyone can afford, they just need to afford love and support and care for the child. The parents get trapped trying to satisfy society by giving the child what the child doesn't even care about. At age five a child doesn't fully comprehend rich and poor, however they are able to comprehend when their purpose is invalidated. They end up seeking attention, they start acting in ways they too are not comfortable with, but instead of parents realizing this, they continue to smack the child, reprimand the child and tell the child that they are worthless.

A child is programmed from a young age that whatever their parents say is the way, it is right, it is the only way. Children are beaten, discouraged, and called names when their instinct reminds them who they are. The act of listening to parents is not at all wrong, it is part of growing up. What many parents have instilled however is NO. They have used their power of guidance to reprimand their children by limiting their ability to excel. Parents only speak to their children to reprimand them, they instill failure, disadvantage, and inadequacy into the minds of the young. You see this when a child shows their artistic ambitions by drawing on the walls, the parents bring a belt, beat the child, and says, "What will my friends say if my house has crayon on its walls? You are always messing. What is your problem? I don't know when you will stop all this nonsense." Or when the child expresses their musical interest and sings along to music and their parent says, "Listen here I am watching my favorite drama, can you shut up, can't you hear that you are making a noise? I will smack you if you make that noise one more time." Or when a child spends time at the gym practicing their favorite sport and they come home late from practice and their parent says, "I will beat you, why are you home this late? Who do you think is supposed to wash the dishes if you are not here? I don't care what sport nonsense you want to do, when I say come back to do work in this house, you stop all that sport nonsense and come back to do your chores." Or when a child stays up all night studying and keeps the house lights on to try and study the parent says, "Can't you see we are trying to sleep? Switch the lights off and go sleep." These children get programmed to think that their abilities are invalid. They have also been programmed to do everything their parents tell them, and yes, they stop drawing, they stop singing, they stop athletics, they stop achieving academically. They stop pursuing their purpose. You need to let go of the things that have been said to you that question your value. There are things that you were told or heard about you that have undermined the sense of self love and appreciation that you had for yourself as a child. There were things said to you that discouraged you from fully being comfortable with who you are.

"You are not beautiful," these four words have crippled and damaged a lot of people. I struggled with my self-image growing up because I heard this a lot in primary school. I was told

I was not beautiful, and it took me a long time to be comfortable with myself and most importantly to love myself. It affected my confidence and deterred me from loving myself. It might seem small but there is a lot of power that is associated in how you see yourself based on what society says. There is a high association to how you see yourself and how confident you are. I say infiltrated because this phrase hurts a lot of people who end up not being able to confront what is in the mirror. For you to find your purpose and the pleasure of your purpose you need to be very confident with what you see in the mirror. Society's narrative of beauty has crippled many souls, but now it is time to let go. There is something about what you see in the mirror and what you tell what you see in the mirror. When you look in the mirror there is a level of connection that you have with yourself. When you look at yourself there is a deep unexplainable connection that connects you with your soul. Which is why it's important to remove all what society has said about the way you look, let go of everyone's beauty standard. The reason why I say to let go is because the first step to knowing your purpose is that you must be able to see yourself, connect with yourself with the true pure beauty that is your soul. Look at yourself in full confidence and assurance of what you see, not doubting what you see, but marveling at the idea that you have a purpose like no one else. You are special, the way you look, how you feel, how you think and how you act is exclusive to you and to you alone. How you see yourself is essential to the conversations that you have with yourself. You need to let go of every negative view that you have of yourself that has been influenced by society. See yourself in your purest form, which is who you are. Be comfortable with what you see in the mirror, love what you see, connect with what you see, comfort what you see, embrace what you see, speak to what you see because what you see is the beauty of God's hands and the beauty of you, which no one can take away from you.

The thing about the feeling of finding your purpose is that it makes sense, it puts everything and life itself into perspective. It makes life make sense. You become a spiritual being connected to your Maker. You radiate when exercising your purpose, you are happy when exercising your purpose. I wish I could find the proper vocabulary to explain the feeling. This feeling connects you to the power God rested in you. Unfortunately, we let things distract us, we allow fear and society to define what our purpose is. We are always discussing words like wealth and money and those things are not really connected with the inner being, the soul. They provide materialistic value that has no connection whatsoever with the inner being. I have recently developed reservations to the phrase, "Dreaming big." I have always emphasized this concept, and I still do even later in the book, as to what is necessary to finding the true meaning of life. This changed as I realized that we are programmed to dream big, and the propaganda dream is one that doesn't necessarily connect the outer man with the inner man. Society makes us believe that the dream is having a car, a house, taking your children to the "best" school and settling in a job that will pay your bills until you die. Many people have made this their purpose. Many get to work hard at reaching this "dream." When they get that degree, they have the well-paying job, they have the nice house, the car, the spouse, the children, the designed life. Then they realize that they are not satisfied, they are not happy. They then work hard to try and perhaps get a better position, thinking that perhaps more money will satisfy whatever void they have. Years go by and that person is still not happy, not satisfied, and finds it difficult to connect to their soul. I am not saying that everyone who is wealthy is not living a purposeful life, neither am I saying your purpose won't bring you success and wealth, but I wish you may experience the beauty of your purpose. *Your* purpose, not the one sold to you by the architects of capitalism. No one in this world has the same purpose as you because of the following reasons:

1. You are unique. You can be inspired and motivated by someone, but no one in this world has the same purpose as you. Your distinct print (your fingerprint) is the tag and barcode to your purpose. Each barcode is different because each product is independent to the other even though they might be the same product. So, you can have a similar goal. Perhaps you and your friend are both aspiring to be doctors, which is amazing, you might be in the same class, have the same marks, graduate on the same day, but you are different doctors, because you are two products, two

different people. You might work in the same practice, you might use the same products, but because God has given the two friends different barcodes you are two different products. Let's make it simple. Two breads, both white, sitting on the shelf. These two breads are both identical on the shelf. The one loaf is taken first, and the other loaf sits there waiting, eventually it is also bought by its new owner. Something we first need to see is that the bread's journeys out of the store happened at different times by two different owners, both the same brand, same packaging, exactly identifiable breads. The second thing is that both these breads serve a different purpose. The one might be bought as the only food that could be afforded, it is eaten for supper, breakfast, and lunch with butter and oros.

2. The other loaf is bought to be a base for a new recipe that will be included in a table with a 7-color meal. These loaves are identical, different barcodes, different purposes. That is the same thing with our lives. We might look the same, be of the same background, but that doesn't mean that we will identify our purpose at the same time. Also, we won't serve the same purpose. God gets highly disappointed when we actively seek to succumb to the standards of the world in order to have what we are made to believe is living. LIVING IS CONNECTING YOUR INNER MAN AND OUTER MAN. You are given the responsibility to

discover who the inner man is. You are created to live a purpose. Your purpose is going to make and fulfill God's plan for the world. Imagine if everyone opened their hearts to being what God says they are and what they could be. There would be harmony and happier human beings connected to their true self. You unfortunately won't be able to tap into the realization of what exactly it is that you are meant to be if you don't connect to God as He will reveal the purpose. Your purpose is supposed to bring God glory. God has given us all we need to succeed. God has blessed us with nature. Everything we see and have as humanity was sourced from nature. Therefore, God has given us resources that will ensure that we strive in the pursuit of purpose. He has given us intelligence, skill, and talents to make use of these resources. The conversation then soon became about power. God has given us dominion and power over the nature and everything in this world. God breathed Himself within us. We have God, the inventor, the founder, the creator, the maker inside of us. Therefore, that means that we too can do all those things. Our purpose is in that power. Once we tap into that power, we are unstoppable. Only those willing to access that power will reap the benefits of their purpose.

Never allow the pain of your past block you from realizing your purpose. There are so many things that happen to every one of us, but your purpose is still your purpose. Perhaps your purpose will not take you out of whatever situation you might be in, but surely your purpose will ensure that your heart is content.

CHAPTER 3

PRINCIPLES TO LIVE A PURPOSEFUL LIFE

1.   Love

THIS IS THE MOST IMPORTANT PRINCIPLE. LOVE IS THE MOST precious gift that you can give to someone, including yourself. You were created to love. You were created to give love, get love, and be loved. As humans we cannot live independent of love because we are emotional beings and therefore one of the reasons you were created was to ensure that there is continuous outflow and inflow of love. There are various definitions that are associated with love. The love that I am talking about is the one that reaches to change someone else's life. You are created therefore, to give out that love and receive that love. The same amount of love being like the one that you develop for your purpose. The love is innate, and many people have managed to suppress that love and passion. Unfortunately, the ability to love any other way is associated with how you have chosen to love your purpose and place value in that purpose. We ask ourselves why there is so little love? The reason is that people do not know any other way to portray their frustration of not living in their purpose. There is nothing that can substitute this frustration; the more frustration you build up, the less you show love.

There are two types of love that you should give.

a.   Love to others

It is difficult to live in the world without giving or receiving love. Love elevates the ordinary human experience to the unexplainable measure of humanity. Love is necessary, and everyone deserves to be loved. You need to love and be loved in order to find a sense of completion. No one can say that they do not need love. There are different relationships we have as humans, but the level of love shared depends on the amount of trust, care, and connection to the other person. Love for family, partners and friends is innate, it is bound to happen, it is automatic, not programmed, but authentic. You need to start sharing love to those outside the circle you believe to love. Share love with humanity. Share love to those you do not know. There is satisfaction and peace that you feel when you have exchanged the simplest form of being a human. Love is the simplest form. One can be stripped of every material thing they possess, however if they have love around them, they are able to survive because love is all you need. There is a human connection that activates the human in the other person when they receive love. Love is internal, and the other person will feel or connect with your love when receiving it. In order to find your purpose or go about living a purposeful life you need to share love, give love, and receive love. I put this principle first because it is the simplest principle. Share love, let your presence represent and express love. We are created to live together whilst sharing love to create a harmonious society. We do not need all we think we need to live amongst each other, we do not need to be anything, we just need to love each other. It is your responsibility to give love. Be the kind of person that can be identified with humanity. Understand other people as humans. Do not discriminate, do not hate but love another human because they are a human. Your heart will be clear, your heart finds joy when you appreciate someone for them being human. Growing up I was exposed to different types of people, different races, and classes. I lived in a very poor area, struck by extreme poverty, however everyone loved each other. One thing that made everyone survive in the presence of nothing was love. Because there was nothing else to value, they valued each other, and to some extent that is enough. Some of the people did not get the pleasure of discovering their purpose, but they had the biggest part in their hearts fulfilled through sharing and receiving love. They laughed, shared memories, and had love.

b.   Love for yourself.

This is my favorite because it cannot be mimicked or performed. You need to have a great level of self-love in order to desire or want to discover your purpose. There is nothing more satisfying than giving yourself a gift, the gift being your purpose. In order to have any of the other principles in perspective you need to value and love yourself. The other principles all make sense because you have given yourself enough love and value. You must love yourself enough to find what it is your soul desires. Your purpose has challenges and obstacles, and in order to find strength to overcome those, you need to be confident in the love you have for yourself. Love everything about yourself. Embrace everything about you, from your strengths to your weaknesses and celebrate yourself for being you. Love how you look, how you sound, your personality, and everything else because it makes you who you are.

2.   Care

We are living in a time of "IDC- I don't care" and "Whatever." This principle is difficult to express because through globalization, people meet people they don't know or have ever met and that doesn't ignite the passion to care because you do not know anyone and don't have to know them. The principle of caring is simple, care. May there never be the absence of help in your presence, be the initiator to bring about change in every problem there is in front of you. Being purposeful is being able to connect with other humans on a humanly level. It is not easy, but it is necessary, and being able to care for others is another principle of purpose that not everyone can access. The attitude of "I don't care" is not sustainable because just like others need your help, so do you need theirs. We often pretend we do not need other people, but we need each other more than we can imagine. This principle is to remind and encourage everyone to care because ultimately our humanly being always prevails and not having that humanly experience is what is driving humanity apart. The root of not caring for each other is another book for another day. However, we need to start caring for each other. The level of depression and suicide is increasing because as humans we have decided to separate ourselves from what makes us a community. We all don't care about each other, even though we are slowly dying. We need to constantly be there for each other, check up on one another and show empathy at all times. Therefore, in order to be purposeful, you need to care about yourself by caring for others. Caring does not necessarily mean giving someone something, but just the thought of good things upon someone else, calling someone else just to ask how they are doing, telling someone they are beautiful, telling someone you love them, telling someone well done. Any gesture that shows that you are thinking about that person. A smile, to some is all you need to express to show them that you care.

Care is a principle because life is not all about you. Part of your purpose is making other people feel human by accessing that humanity and giving it to them. You also feel good when exercising care. Care does not come at any cost, but it rewards your soul tremendously.

3.   Prayer/ Meditation

Pray until something happens. Pray when there is something, pray when there is nothing. You need to understand that there is a higher power bigger than you. I pray, not because of anything, but just because I believe I owe my being to God. Therefore I need to constantly acknowledge Him. I believe that for us to connect with the power inside of us, we need to be in constant communication and in order with the one who made us. Going back to Genesis 1:26-28, which states, "Let us make humankind in our own image, according to our likeness and let them have domination over the fish of the sea, and the birds of the air, and over the cattle, and over every creeping thing that creeps on the earth." Then verse 27 continues to state, "So God created humankind in his image, in the image of God he created them," and 28 continues, " God blessed them, and God said to them, 'Be fruitful and multiply, and fill the earth and subdue it; and have dominion over the fish of the sea and over the birds of the air and over every living creature that moves upon the earth." We can see in those couple of verses how powerful we are. Being given dominion by the Maker of the universe must mean that we are pretty special. I believe that God has given us everything to ensure that we at our maximum. He has given us Godliness.

Sometimes we forget that we are powerful, that we are made to dominate. Constant communication and connection with God are important to fuel that power that does not seize to end. I believe that prayer is the one personal thing that connects you to your soul. Some may call it meditation, but it is important that you take the time to connect from your source of life in order to find meaning in life. Prayer guides you, it saves you from making bad decisions because if you pray there is a level of guidance that you get. We must remember that we do not have it all figured out, we need a higher power to guide us and show us direction. Let us not forget to pray, it's free, therefore do it and feel the liberation of being connected to your soul whilst connecting with God. He is also a listener and is there when you feel tired, heavy, and defeated, through prayer you will find strength. Do not give up, just pray about it.

4.   Laughter

This is one of the most overlooked things ever. Laughter is such a liberating feeling. We are a very serious generation. We have been made to believe that we need to constantly be serious for things to go well. Sometimes you need to just be chilled and laugh about it. I find myself laughing at the most difficult situations not because I am unaware of the seriousness of the moment, but just because I realized that being sad and depressed about it won't bring about solutions. Laugh, be happy and never ever allow anyone to take that happiness away from you. I realized that happiness needs to come from the inside. You need to find peace inside your heart, peace and joy that transcends in the presence of difficulty. Challenges should never take away your joy and peace. You can do better in a peaceful and calm state of being than a state of panic. You need to always strive to find that inner sense of peace that will help you make proper decisions. Laugh, be happy, you only live once, do everything you love, be with people you love and laugh a lot. Free yourself from the chains bound to trap you in dark holes of depression and anxiety.

5.   Dream Big

I am always fascinated by the true concept of dreaming; I think it is very beautiful. I would consider myself as a dreamer. I say this because I love to think of the impossible and dream of perhaps all those becoming a reality. I dream of the most abstract, unthought of things, like how we can go about eradicating poverty in Africa, how can we instill self-confidence and self-love upon black children? I dream of an Africa that is mentally revolutionized, a transformed Africa that affords Africans a stern voice that speaks as the world listens. My biggest dream is to eradicate poverty in Africa. This dream might *seem* impossible, but it is possible. Dream the unreachable, dream so big that those around you call you crazy. Also never get to a point where you stop dreaming. Never get to a point where you are not dreaming anymore. If you stop dreaming you will settle for any and everything. Never feel that you are too old to dream, never get tired of dreaming. Dream big, work hard and you will succeed. Never allow your dream to be determined by society. Dreaming about only having a car, a house and lots of money is not necessarily a dream because anyone can have those. A dream is what seems impossible, unreachable, but possible, it is the actions of your purpose coming into manifestation.

6.   Forgiveness

Forgiveness is one of the most difficult things to do for us as humans. It is, however, necessary for us to live effective purposeful lives. Forgiveness is the voluntary decision of the victim (who's been hurt) to release resentment towards the person, group or situation that hurt them. The natural, normal thing to do would be to resent anyone who's hurt you. However, forgiveness offers a different alternative. It is the act of letting go. Actively deciding that you want to let go of the feeling of the pain the person, group or situation caused. If you think about it, if you have not forgiven that person, you are bound to relieve the pain and hurt they have caused you. The key to a peaceful soul and heart, is one that lets go of any feeling or emotion that continuously brings pain. I am not saying that we must be immune to feelings or emotions. If you are hurt you must feel pain, but what I am saying is that at a certain point you need to release the pain and allow peace and serenity inside your soul. Instead of holding on to the pain, use it to your advantage. Every pain, problem or challenge you go through you are to learn something and be a better person filled with experience and knowledge because of that pain. Therefore, if someone has hurt you, for example, instead of hating or resenting that person, you might as well introspect and identify what lesson you have learnt from when the person did you right or wrong. We often like to offer other people the privilege to be entitled to our journey's, remember that you decide what you make of every pain. Now as I was saying, every time you feel like you have been hurt, ask yourself the following questions in order to channel the motivation for forgiveness.

a. What lesson am I learning from this experience? Every painful experience is to produce beautiful results. It is easier to understand when it's in most cases but one so painful to understand is being hurt by people you love. However, it is essential that sometimes you get hurt by those people because you will learn some principles from the experience of separation. You learn independence, for example. You might be disappointed by relationships that fail, as a result of the other person initiating the end of the relationship, not fully understanding that just maybe you were too dependent on the person, whether it be for happiness or money, you perhaps depended on this person for everything, and it was time that you learnt the importance of being your own person. Every painful experience is to make us stronger and wiser people. Those experiences are there to make you stronger, therefore be cognizant of the new strength you are about to receive from that painful experience.

b. Why did this person/ group/ situation do this to me? They did it to you perhaps because you were meant to go through that. Never despise painful situations or challenges because only those who survive those can be labeled as strong, courageous, brave, and powerful. Only those who can conquer through storms are named victorious. Perhaps it has happened to you because you are meant to be great. Perhaps it has happened to you because there is power in you! You had a challenge that needed to be conquered in order to fully exercise that greatness.

c. What contribution did I have?

We are a society that never wants to take responsibility. Most times we are in positions of pain because we put ourselves in them, but do not worry, that is also part of your journey. We are hurt by people because we ourselves have given them the power to do so, which is why I emphasize the importance of first being content with yourself, your actions, and your purpose. Once you are content with yourself, you do not allow people to hurt you. There are instances where we have no control, and people hurt us without us expecting or anticipating it. Sometimes we give people the right to hurt us. We allow people the advantage of dictating our lives, which is where we need to take a pause and ask ourselves why. This goes back to introspection. Once you are happy with yourself, you do not depend on other people for happiness because the minute that person takes away the happiness they brought, it becomes difficult to forgive them. Please do not think I am saying you should blame yourself for being hurt, however don't allow anyone trying to hurt you to win. Be so content with yourself that no one can take you or break you when they decide to hurt you. So yes, others have brought pain to you, but you are well responsible for how far that hurt goes. Dwell in your serenity,

The reason why we do not ask ourselves these questions is because we avoid introspection. Being able to forgive takes a lot of self-work. It takes a lot of the inner self being settled. In order to be truly settled and not shaken by other people's actions towards you, you are able to forgive them. You should be able to stand up for your serenity. Being able to forgive means you have spent enough time with yourself to fully understand the importance of not allowing other people in your serenity. Forgiveness is being comfortable with yourself and the obstacles presented to you. It is knowing that it will not always be smooth sailing. Associate every pain to being just a mere obstacle, that most times you need to learn or grow from. Yes, pain is part of growing. Our biggest mistake is wanting things to go a certain way, our way, and when they do not, we blame everyone who we believe is responsible for things not going a certain way. Forgiveness is saying, "I thank you for every contribution you have added to my life because if you didn't do what you did, I would have not been where I am today." Sometimes it is not people that hurt us, but there are two other ways of being hurt and we also need to forgive these:

1.   Forgive situations.

There are certain situations and circumstances that we often blame and resent as we believe that if things had turned out differently, we would have been happier. Some situations we are born into, many people think that perhaps if they were born in a different family or situation perhaps their lives would have been better. You were born into that family or situation for a reason therefore the sooner you accept that, the sooner you will realize that blessing because those who are powerful arise from the hardest of pain. Perhaps if you came from that family you wish you were from, you would have not been as strong as you are. You would not become the person you are today, and in order to find joy in what you are presented with is to forgive that situation. Forgive the situation that you found yourself in when you got hurt. Forgive the situation because the situation was meant to be, do not despise that. Forgive your background, forgive the family you were born to, forgive the school you went to, forgive every situation that brought pain to you. You are able to create better situations and environments for yourself once you forgive those that brought upon discomfort and pain to you. Forgive them, channel your heart to serenity.

2.   Forgive yourself.

Forgive yourself for the pain you have caused yourself. Forgive yourself for allowing your heart to be bitter. Forgive yourself for not trusting yourself, for not believing in you. Forgive yourself for not forgiving. Forgive yourself for blaming others. Forgive yourself for not taking responsibility. Forgive yourself for not wanting to spend time with yourself. Forgive yourself for not allowing your purpose to occur. Forgive yourself for not taking responsibility for making your dreams come through. Forgive yourself for not being patient with yourself. Forgive yourself for not loving yourself. Forgive yourself for not giving yourself space from the rest of the world. Forgive yourself for allowing negative energy into your life. Forgive yourself for bringing pain to other people. Forgive yourself for entertaining toxicity in your life. Forgive yourself for giving into temptations that distracted you. Forgive yourself for not having enough confidence, for not trusting yourself. Forgive yourself.

Research proves that unforgiveness is one of the causes of certain health issues. Unforgiveness is not only detrimental to your physical health but also to your mental, emotional, and spiritual health. Many people seem fine, look fine and pretend to be okay. However, when they are alone, the darkness of ill-health blocks them, and they suffer buried in the heap of darkness. Forgiveness frees you from both physical and mental diseases. Forgiveness sets you free. Your spirit becomes free and is let loose. It is not easy, but it is beneficial for your own sanity. The thing about unforgiveness is that the person you are holding in your heart is not the one set bound by the chains of darkness, you are. Therefore, let go, let that person go, that situation, that pain, let it go. You deserve to be happy, you deserve to be free. The greatest gift you can give yourself is self-love, and to fully love yourself means protecting your soul, what comes in it and what you block from it. Your true self is your soul, therefore protect that soul as you have the power to block and allow anything to enter, therefore you can decide not to allow pain, anger and unforgiveness to dwell in your heart. Embrace yourself and love yourself, forgive yourself.

7.   Integrity

Integrity is one of the most important principles as it is sure to sustain you throughout and bring value to your life. It is particularly difficult when it has not been shown to you. Some of us are not born in the most "well-structured" families or the most "well-put together" communities, therefore we do not fully recognize nor can relate to the concept of integrity. It is however, just in a manner of channeling something already inside of you. To some extent, I believe that actually the greatest integrity can be found in the face of the adversity that we grew up in; integrity being the ability to survive in the midst of the brokenness of our families and communities. I say this because where I was born and raised, it was the ability to wake up early in the morning, get dressed and go work hard to provide food for your children that bestowed the honor of integrity. I believe that the greatest form of integrity is in the ability to find joy and love in the presence of poverty and brokenness. There is another level of power that you need to access in order to have the hunger to want to live another day in the presence of adversity. The applaudable men and women who wake up early in the morning to prepare to polish and maintain their integrity. I say this because you have to be clothed with the greatness of integrity in order to be able to put aside your passions, inspirations, and dreams in order to give your time in service of another person in order to make their lives easier, you are doing this in order to maintain your integrity and promise to your children to provide for them. I think that is the greatest level of integrity. So as much as that form of integrity may be looked down upon and shamed, it is the greatest!

In order to understand integrity, you need to be able to understand honesty. That disadvantaged parent doing everything they can to provide for their children is staying true to their promise to nurture their offspring. Therefore, integrity is being honest and sticking to your word. Being honest is highly essential to living a life of purpose because your purpose requires honesty. You need to be honest with the following people:

1. Yourself

   The first person you need to show integrity to is yourself. You need to embed integrity within your daily living. A guilty conscience comes when you have disturbed your integrity. You feel it when you have stepped out of bound to the borders of what is your personal integrity. Others extend or reduce their level of self-integrity, by choice. You are not taught self-integrity. It can be modelled to you, but you initially decide how you wish to bound your integrity. Your guilty conscious then speaks to the humanly element of you and you decide to comfort or discard your guilty conscious. With a multiplication of consciousness discarded, the person then does actions that may be to the detriment of their integrity. There is great power in embracing your humanly element of integrity. Integrity makes YOU a person that can be trusted. Being trusted and admired boosts your esteem and sense of morale. Being able to stand firm towards your truth is integrity. The reason why I say integrity to yourself is important, is because you are accountable for being integral to your purpose. You need to be accountable for the choices you decide to make, whether to move towards or away from your purpose. Being true and honest to yourself is showing yourself the utmost integrity. No one can bestow this form of integrity on you. You display the highest level of integrity towards yourself if you choose to acknowledge the reason for your existence. You owe yourself that much love and passion to discover your true purpose. You need to show yourself the greatest level of respect by being honest in your dreams and purpose. You deserve to be honest with yourself before anyone else. Integrity is also being able to maintain and uphold that truth. Once you have been able to withstand and maintain what it is that you are meant to do and who you are, you are integral. Integrity for you is integrity with your inner self, no one provides honor to this integrity, but once you have maintained it you are able to live at peace with yourself, you are internally satisfied.

2. Your generation and family

This is the second important because your decisions and honesty with yourself, who you are and what you are meant to be will affect your generation. Your generation is a product of the person you chose to be today, the legacy you leave behind your name. When you choose to stay true to yourself, your generation benefits because they receive the best version of you. The best version of you is the one that lived a purposeful life. This is not specific to monetary value, it is based in the true essence of who you are, the best you. Integrity can be a baton handed to generations to sustain and withhold your future generations. You want to be remembered for something great. The greatest thing is being able to live a purposeful life that can be modelled by others, filled with integrity. Being honest to your generation is allowing God's plan to prevail because if your purpose is driven by Him, who is all-knowing, meaning He will be able to know your future generation, and who to be in order to fulfill His plan of your generation. You owe your future the integrity inside of you because that integrity will drive you to discovering your ultimate purpose to help produce your generation. When you are born into a specific family, the minute you are born you are accepting the responsibility to be a member of that family, therefore being able to withhold the integrity is being able to carry the integrity of that family. You need to therefore be able to discern your purpose for that family so that you can be able to take an integral role into manifesting it for the betterment and enhancement of the family.

Integrity is embraced with honor. Once you display integrity you are respected, loved, embraced, honored, looked after, and blessed. Just like we display great honor to our mothers who worked extremely hard to fulfill their promise to raise us, you will be honored for walking and staying in truth. Staying in the truth of your purpose no matter what challenge and circumstance you face. With no promise of an absence of difficulty in the splendor of integrity, it is however promised to present the power of purpose. The ability to maintain that integrity is where the true power lies. Have integrity, not to please anyone, but may it be in your DNA as it becomes part of your life.

8. CONFIDENCE

Confidence is the key factor that can either make or break your purpose. Confidence is not necessarily the ability to stand in front of people or the ability to do certain things that other people cannot do, confidence is the mere ability to say Yes, and No. A confident person is someone who is comfortable with decisions that they make and are unapologetic about them. The reason why confidence is a principle is because you have to be able to say yes and no in the journey of purpose. You have to say yes to your purpose. That inner voice that tells you this is what you are supposed to do, or this is who you are supposed to be. You have to say Yes to who you are meant to be. You have to say yes to your ambitions, yes to your dreams. You have to say yes to the power inside you that ignites your passion. You have to say Yes to you. Then you are confident. You are also confident when you are able to say NO. You have to say No to distractions, say no to negativity. The ability to say NO to everything that will deter you from reaching and maximizing your purpose. Confidence is standing up for what is right for you no matter who says what. Confidence is what makes some people strong and some people weak. The strong are firm in their decisions, they do not waiver around, but are very aware of what they want and what they do not. Their Yes is Yes, and No is No. People without confidence are unsure about what they want, who they are and what they are meant to do. We all have the potential to be confident, we just need to be very aware of what we want and not change that because of people. Be confident. Say Yes, Say No and do not apologize for it.

REJECTION

I HOSTED AN EVENT TO LAUNCH A VIDEO FOR A CAMPAIGN that I shot with 16 few young professionals. I had about 30 people, who I had trusted, that confirmed their availability for the event, and they did not come, only about 10 people came. As I watched the people not walking in the door, a beautiful thought came to my mind. I realized the beauty of being rejected by people. There are two types of rejection from people:

1. General rejection.

   There are various levels of this kind of rejection because they mean different things to different people depending on which stage you are in life. This is the one that is seen when someone rejects you on Facebook or when you do not get that promotion that you want from work. You feel pain, frustration, and anger for a very short space of time because you soon realize that you can then again later achieve those things perhaps by trying harder. And here are more examples that can be seen in this rejection:

- Rejection from your family for breaking a cup.
- Rejection from your teacher when asking something.
- Rejection from a friend by not answering your text.

This kind of rejection is one that you can easily recover from. This rejection can be easily replaced by something else. You can replace your disappointment about your rejected Facebook request by inviting someone else who will most likely accept that request. You can buy another cup and replace the one you broke, and your family could get over it.

Everyone goes through General rejection, it could happen anytime, anywhere. It happens, you move on and just around the corner you get what you were rejected for. Your heart pounds at a temporary base because you can find the recovery very soon. This rejection is okay. You find people to support you as you get through it. When you cry, they assist you. When you are feeling low because of the rejection, they pick you up, hold your hand and walk with you. This rejection is part of being human, it's normal. It is a form of rejection that is part of growing up, everyone goes through it.

2.   Expedient Rejection

The word "Expedient" means something convenient, it can be referenced from the idea as being "to one's advantage." There is extensive advantage in this rejection because it cannot be replaced. You find advantage from this rejection because nothing you do or say will remove this rejection. This form of rejection makes you feel that you ought to be in gruesome pain. Find your feet in that pain and work to survive through this rejection. Not everyone understands this rejection, not everyone goes through this rejection. This kind of rejection is for the world's greatest. This rejection is one that cannot be recovered, it is one that refines you. Just like heat refines gold, this heat makes you stronger, it makes you bolder. This is the kind of rejection where you find yourself alone. You find yourself in a space where you are alone and rejected by everyone. Family members, friends, and everyone you know suddenly become strangers. It is a space where you feel like you are deserted by the world. You feel like the whole world is against you. You try your best to understand why it is happening to you. You get this kind of rejection when you are YOU. You get this rejection when you are confident in your true self. You experience it when you are not apologetic about who you are. Many people do not understand why you are so honest in your self expression. There are phases that you go through if you are someone who is imparted with the gift of greatness. In every phase, people reject you until there are very few people left, if any:

a. You discover that you are ambitious, you cannot sleep at night because there is something that burns inside of you. You have this desire to be great, you share this desire with someone you trust well enough and hope they will further fuel this by motivating you. Instead, you start seeing that person distancing themselves from you. You start questioning what it is that is making that person behave in a diminishing manner towards you. You stop telling and stop trying to pursue this passion you have. Finally, everyone gets back to loving you because they see that you have reverted to being the uninspired you, the you that comforts in the inability to identify your passion, the normal you. You are then integrated back into normality because you are part of a collective uninspired, demotivated, un-ambitious group. You are then part of the normal community. You choose a career path that everyone else is doing, you dress the way everyone dresses, you speak the way everyone speaks, you do what everyone else does because you are part of the community. There are people who stay in this phase for the rest of their lives and because of this everyone likes them because they chose to settle. Once you refuse to be in this phase, you go to the next stage.

b. A few find themselves in the second phase. This phase is where you find a lot of discomfort in the pleasures of the first phase. You cannot sleep at night, this passion just ignites more fire inside of you. You just continue feeling like you cannot comprehend why you are the one that is being taunted by the idea of greatness. You then ignore the people that do not motivate you in your passions. You continue to live your passions and slowly start seeing the benefits of being unapologetically you. You then find people who are as passionate as you are, and who also , have passed through phase one. You then find support from these people. You all support each other's hustle and try to achieve your ambitions. You walk together until you start seeing the benefits of your hustle. It gets difficult when the people you are hustling with do not get the opportunities and experiences that you receive. They start rejecting and distancing themselves from you. Now you already had the people who left you in phase one, and now you have people who leave you in phase two. You find it very hard to understand because you thought that these people were the ones who were going to stand with you. You then have few people around you, less people to hold your hand when you do fail. You realize that there is no one to pick you up. Just like in phase one, the hardship of rejection becomes too much. Others stay hustling and hustling until they find themselves back in stage one. Others decide to go to the next phase, despite the rejection and pain they experience.

c.   This stage is what we can identify as the true epitome of success. Unfortunately, chances of being alone and lonely are high in this phase. As the saying goes, "The higher you go, the colder it becomes." In this instance it means that you feel the pain and rejection even more, alone. This kind of rejection is one where you have a lot of people surrounding you for various reasons, some to benefit from you, some to bring you down. You continue to feel the coldness of this phase as many say they can no longer associate with you because of their predetermined idea of someone who is confident and assertive in their choices and decisions to fulfill their purpose. People tend to pre-judge you and have preconceptions about you that can hurt you or bring down your sense of confidence. When people say, "Success has changed him/her," you need to evaluate and introspect. You need to introspect whether your attitude and character has changed, or people are misinterpreting you. If you find yourself to think less of those who have not reached this phase because of the pressures associated with the power of success, then do bring about change in how you view them. It does not matter what everyone else thinks about you, as long as you align your character with the humanity within you, trust your power and your inner being. This phase requires a lot of responsibility, strength, and courage. This level takes a level of purpose maturity, which is not associated with age, but with strength, a strong level of faith and courage. This level does not require you to be anything but yourself. It maximizes the true potential that we all possess as humans. It brings it out and radiates it in alignment of your true meaning to existence. This level does not necessarily equate to being materially rich, that is going to happen automatically. This level means connection with yourself on all levels. This level means understanding why you are on Earth, why you are alive and what contribution you have to the world. Being in this phase means you took it upon yourself to ignore all social ills and journeyed to find your true sense of being. It is very difficult to get to this phase and takes a great level of focus. Some might say their childhood has shaped them to align them to this phase, some might say the difficulty of their childhood motivated them to get to this phase, some might say their faith helped guide them to this phase, some might say that their confidence pushed them to this phase. I believe that every human being has the potential and power to access this phase, every human being however needs to realize this power whilst allowing this phase to manifest as their glory in the reason for their existence.

CHAPTER 5

THE FEAR OF REJECTION

PEER PRESSURE STEMS FROM THE IDEA OF FEAR OF REJEC-tion. The pressure that comes from the fear of rejection then spirals to uniformity and identifying with a social construct, that construct then becomes a norm. The norm becoming the society. As human beings we are born with the desire and need to be loved. The fear of being alone is what makes most people succumb to what everyone else is doing so that they are not left alone. You need to adapt an attitude of being okay with yourself enough to not worry about who or what will leave you. Spend as much time as you can with yourself to be able to indoctrinate yourself with your purpose. This will direct people who are aligned to your purpose and those who think and reason similarly to the way you do. In the beginning it does get hard because this passion you have starts changing the way you think.

For a long time, I used to ask myself, what is wrong with me? For a long time, I used to question whether there was something I was doing wrong that pushed the world away. I was lonely, and no one really wanted to be friends with me. There was a time where I despised being around other people because no matter how hard I tried, there was no group of people that I could fit in with. When I would try and express myself, people either laughed and ridiculed me, or would never want to talk to me again. With this experience I began to understand that type of rejection was preparing me for the No's that I constantly received after that. I then began looking at rejection from a different perspective.

Someone once asked me how I got into Mcing, well the story goes as follows: In High school teachers were never fond of me, and for me it was okay because unfortunately, for them, they didn't realize that their rejection was driving me to my purpose. I used to audition for roles in our high school plays and musicals and every time I auditioned, I did not get the roles. Every time there was a production, I would not be given a role. I would be given a role of being at the back as a back-up dancer or extra. I decided that since they do not want me to act on stage, I would ask the teachers if they could let me MC and introduce the plays as they come on stage at least. At the time it did not seem like an important role to do because the most important people were the actors.

So, I asked to take the role of introducing the most important people. I was highly honored by this and I really enjoyed it. What I decided to do was not to give up on the passion of being on stage, but to use that rejection to find the positivity in it. I am glad that I was rejected as an actor because now I get to do something that I thoroughly enjoy, which is MCing. Never allow rejection to deter you from your destiny. I now see rejection as positive reinforcement, it means you are doing something different, it means you are bringing about a revolution. It depends on you, whether or not you will do something about seeing the "positive" from the rejection.

I look at the rejection I received from my father, at first, I was angry at him for not taking care of me and not being there to fulfill his role of being a father, however, I had to understand that perhaps it was only through him leaving that my mom was able to meet an amazing man who is now an amazing stepfather to me. If I did not receive rejection from my father, I would not have spent much time with the father that I now know and would have not learnt so much knowledge from him. Perhaps my "real father" would have not allowed me the opportunities and support that my stepfather gave me to make me the strong woman that I am today. Take a close look at your rejection, whatever shape or form you received it, think for a while if you would have gained more insight or known this much if you did not go through that rejection. There is a positive lesson that you learn from rejection. These are the lessons that I learnt from rejection:

- No just means "Not now," " We regret to inform you," "NO," "Sorry," those are very powerful terms because all they mean is you might not get it now. This is an opportunity for growth because you learn that you can go back and empower, uplift, and equip yourself with more skills, more knowledge, more growth. It's an opportunity to improve and get better. Instead of seeing it as a no take it as, "okay that means I need to acquire more skill in this area," which possibly would be beneficial for you. This doesn't mean settle for failure, but it simply means don't see rejection as a reason to give up. There is nothing wrong with being disappointed, however there comes a point where you need to use that energy to push you to equip yourself.

  I am someone who has attended hundreds of auditions and callbacks, never receiving any of the roles or parts I was auditioning for. After every audition I would get home and think about ways and research ways to become a better performer.

- There is something special about you if you get rejected. People and society do not reject people who are like them or share the same values and dreams as them. Society rejects those that think outside the box, the innovators, the game-changers, the ones who take initiative, the dreamers, the visionaries. They are the people that are rejected because they are breaking the norm. The norm could be a mindset, a concept that the society is refusing to mentally let go of. If you get rejection from everyone around you, it is because you are different. Embrace that difference and allow the difference to motivate you to become strong enough to resist and stand firm against the pressures of society.

DIARY ENTRY: 30 August 2018

I understand why some give up. I understand why some people just cannot do it anymore! It is always when closest to the end where you feel like you are never going to reach the end. I am so tired, so drained and I feel like there is a big weight on my shoulder. I feel tired, not because I want to, I have energy, always good energy, but now something feels different, something changed. I am at a point and there is something about this point that is very draining yet encouraging. This point is the point where many give up. A point where you ask yourself the question, why me? You are faced with rejection left, right, and center. This point is when no one offers you a hand, a point where no cares. Every time you reach out and seek help, you feel like your hand is being shoved back in the dark place it was in. This is the point where no one believes you, no one believes in you. You hear no after no after no. You ask yourself is it me? What am I doing wrong? Everyone you expect to support you does not support you. My journey makes me cry, it makes me cry every time because it has been difficult, very difficult and continues to be. My journey has been the most challenging journey. No one would understand or comprehend the daily difficulties I face. I cry because I appreciate the strength that God gave me when it was difficult. It has been one that was filled with rejection.

Once you understand the rules of the race you embrace the challenges that come with it. You get embarked with challenges that exceed your capacity. You are left to resolve and find solutions on your own. You experience true rejection and pain at this point. At this point you cry in disappointment because you are not sure how you will get through. This is the point where everyone laughs at you for beginning, everyone says, "I told you so." This point is when your shoulders are so shrunk because your soul, your mind, and heart is tired. It's not necessarily a battle with anyone but yourself. You are battling with your soul, you are battling with your mind. Your head is tired of trying and feels like giving up. You find the motivation to dig deep, reach in and ask yourself important questions. You ask yourself:

- Why did you start this journey?
- Is quitting worth it after working so hard?
- What happens to the long journey I have already travelled?
- What about your hard work? The minute you give up you are disregarding all the hard work you already put in.

I am at a point where I am tired, tired of trying, tired of giving to those around me. Rejection cuts deeply when you are rejected by people that you care about. People you would do anything and everything for. People who you would expect to show you love and support because that is what you have been doing for them. I give, give and give of myself that I receive nothing in return. I care so much, but receive no care in return. I do feel like crying, I feel like bursting into tears, but I will not, I tell myself. I will not cry because I know that I am almost there. I will make it. This is the point that I realize many give up. Many give up at this point. They do not give up because they want to, no one wants to quit what they have started. It is because there does not seem to be help and support. People shut you off as they see you are close to the end. They shut you off because of two things:

1. They do not realize the power of your purpose. They are not aware of how close you are. They do not see or understand your potential, they do not trust your power. You do not seem like someone who can run a marathon. According to their measure, you are weak, you are not strong enough, you are not brave enough. They see your light, but it's not bright enough for them that they don't see the power of it. I understand these people because the problem is not with you, but unfortunately their unawareness. You need time to distance yourself from these people. You need to distance yourself because interactions with these

people remind you of your incompetence. These people are highly draining. As an emerging entrepreneur, speaker, I always try to do projects and events to grow my events portfolio. And I get to work with a lot of people who are tired of helping, tired of assisting, they are tired of giving me a hand because to them I should just give up. I am at a point where whenever I ask for help, the answer is always no. I have received many "Unfortunately" emails. I have been unsuccessful 99% of the times I try. I only receive 0.1 of what I want, what I pray for, what I wish for.

2. They do it because they see the brightness and they want to dim it. They are threatened with the immense power you withhold. They try and dim it in order to be comfortable. Stay away from this energy, you deserve more.

DIARY ENTRY: 1st September 2018

It was my birthday today and the rejection and pain and hurt cut deep inside my heart. I had planned a benefit concert to raise funds and items for young children from impoverished areas. I invited everyone I knew, from school, family, friends, the industry, to social media. And the hall was not even quarter filled. I was so disappointed, people who I had trusted to be there and support me were not, never mind wish me happy birthday. The Norwegian friends I had recently met, six of them, were in the audience, including family, and performers, making it a total of fifteen people in a venue that accommodates 100-150 people. On my birthday I stood there asking myself if these are the only people I have after 20 years of life. My blood father sent me a voice note about his business on this day, not even a happy birthday. That was an expression of rejection, instead of choosing to celebrate me on my birthday, he chose to not. Like many other birthdays he didn't bother.

After thinking hard about it I realized that I didn't need anyone else to attend that event, I didn't need anyone else to wish me happy birthday. The people that did wish me and did attend my birthday were enough. We spend so much time worried and concerned about how little love and support we receive from others. I have learnt to understand that perhaps the love and support I receive from family and the very few friends I have is enough! It is enough, even though I want more or feel I deserve more because I give more. I have enough, and I should settle and be grateful and nurture the love I receive even though it is little. Being grateful is what is necessary to help you appreciate the love and care you have and receive. You are enough, don't spend time focusing on rejection, focus on the love.

CHAPTER 6

JOURNEYS ON YOUR OWN.

L ONELINESS HAS TAUGHT ME SOMETHING ABOUT ISOLATION that is essential to help you grow, and specifically, *forces* your growth.

1. The minute you decide to be different and take a level and step of difference from what you were, you get isolated. Your growth and success will cost you relationships, friendships, and family. You must make the decision to take on the journey on your own. God isolates you from people for Him to walk alone with you. The minute there are people around your time of growth you will not grow in the most effective and

efficient way. You need to be in a place of isolation. For you to know whether you are truly growing and entering the next phase of your life. You don't even have to do much because the people will automatically leave. There are certain people that you love and do not wish to leave, but it would be highly necessary that you do yourself a favor and isolate yourself. There are certain journeys that you need to travel on your own and the journey to growth is often travelled alone.

You do not have to worry or be afraid, you are not alone. You are just in a season where you must be alone and in absolute isolation because people will distract you. People will automatically get uninterested in spending time with you or being in the same space as you. In this season make sure that you spend this time not in despair that all these people have left you, but in rejoice that growth is yet to come. If that process does not help you grow it will break you. Be careful not to let those people break you. There is a high possibility that you will feel lonely, and that feeling is natural, but you need to pass that feeling. That exact feeling is the test because it is uncomfortable and causes many people to give up in their journey. People find themselves giving up in order to be part of a community. It is not easy because the crowds will make you feel like you are meant to belong, and they can do that because there are more of them than you. That is the test, many people have a problem with growing and therefore they do not want you to grow. Protect your growth, protect yourself and isolate yourself.

It is highly dangerous to exist in crowds. As a human you definitely need people, but you do not need to exist in crowds. To exist in crowds is to not see the meaning of life if you do not have anyone around you. You do everything everyone else is doing. You validate your existence, your sense of being from other people. You are motivated by people's approval in order to find meaning. You feel like you on your own cannot make decisions or be in charge of anything and therefore seek out the approval from other people. You settle on other people's dreams and become part of the statistic, one of the million. You dress like everyone else, talk like everyone, do what other people do, love what other people love. The danger of this is that you lose yourself. There are many replicas of people who buy in the system in order to belong. Belonging is comfortable, in order to be part of a community many feel the need and the desire to immerse themselves in part of a society. A crowd has the power to influence you in ways that are not you. Crowds place an identity on you that you know is not yours, but because you want to fit in, you succumb. Crowds will dictate the way you live your life. You don't see your voice as strong enough to stand in isolation and take its power and its position. Existing in crowds is bigger and greater than peer pressure, because peer pressure is by choice and you can easily decide to ignore that pressure and live your life. However when existing in the crowd, you lose yourself until you get to a point where you cannot spend time by yourself, you cannot listen to yourself because you have lost yourself. The opinion of everyone else matters more than yours. For every decision you make you ask yourself the following question:

What will people say?

If you are asking yourself this question, you are still existing in the crowd. Once people matter in the decisions you make, it means you are choosing them over you. You lose who you are, and your purpose is not realized. I have noticed this because I have seen people become different when you spend time with them alone and not in a group setting. The minute you become different when you are around people than when you are on your own then that crowd has influenced you. Some people act more confident when they are with a crowd, that is caused by high levels of low self-esteem. What will people say? One of the most popular statements that deter people from reaching their full potential and eventually their sense of being. If you knew that the people that you are so concerned about do not care about you. In fact, because they have also succumbed to the world, they too are busy dealing with their own insecurities. I once spoke to someone and they shared with me that the abrupt and highly energized, influential persona that they portray is only to mask the deep depression they are facing. This person is very influential, and many people follow him and are entertained by him and want to be with him to feel better about themselves. They seek validation from him, little do they know that he is even more validated by them. He needs them to fill an empty hole inside. This just proves how detrimental the system is. We must therefore leave this system and exist as individuals and not crowds.

You see, pain and hurt can be a cycle if not stopped and guarded before it gets far. You cannot allow hurt people to hurt you. Most times we compromise our values in order to avoid loneliness by being with people that don't have aligned values with us. It is very important that we take full responsibility for the hurt that comes in our lives. We often allow people to hurt us. The minute we stop placing blame on those who hurt us, we must ask ourselves how we allowed those people to hurt us. You see people respond and react to how you treat them, and they treat you the way you allow them to treat you. I learnt that the hard way as I would allow people to treat me anyhow and talk to me anyhow. I became someone that people used and when they are done, they discarded. As a young person who is ambitious, I had a lot of adults who used to treat me that way. They knew I had energy and zeal and most importantly the hunger and drive to want to learn more. They used that for their own benefit and then discarded me once they had used my energy, skill, and time. At 21 I have become a stronger young woman from the mistakes I made and from the experiences I went through and the people that hurt me. I can understand sometimes why it is easier to succumb as a young person. I was struggling with the concept for many years where I was torn between being young and old. My peers did not want to be friends with me because I had a different view to life, in every space I navigated in I never really belonged. In every space I was in I would either be the youngest or the most uninteresting or the most misunderstood. The challenge in being around adults all the time is that you cannot always relate with certain conversations that they have. And in spaces with my peers they can't always relate to conversations that I want to have. I figured that in that sense I need to learn how to spend time with myself most importantly because there is no particular group that I can relate to fully and that is okay. Initially in this book I was not going to share much about my experiences but in this section, I see it fitting to do so, perhaps you can relate to me too. I spent so much time wanting to belong and, in that process, I found myself belonging in spaces that I was not supposed to belong to.

I had to start taking full responsibility for that action and forget other people and deal with self. Perhaps you are not saddened by that person or people hurting you, but you fear the idea of being alone or lonely. Another responsibility you will have to take is asking yourself, who do you allow in your life. Again because of loneliness we often attract people who are not necessarily good to and for us. I used to accept everyone who wanted to be in my life because I was afraid that I would eventually end up alone. I thought that everyone who wants to be around me has good intentions and might want to be genuine friends with me. I realized the hard way that sometimes people have their own intentions for why they want to be around you and when finding out those intentions, I would get so hurt. After thorough introspection I realized that I was *allowing* these people in my life, therefore I am responsible for how they treated me. I believe there are chances of attracting negative energies into your life if you are negative, you attract good if you are good. Perhaps your energy is good and positive, but then the question remains, how do you attract people who are bad for you? Well, it is because of the desperation of constantly wanting people to either validate you or fill the hole inside you. I can say that I attracted those people because I did not want to be alone. It's very unfortunate that those people hurt you, but yes, it is your fault too. I am not saying you must be a robot that is immune to everyone and everything that comes your way. What I am saying is that you have to guard your soul. I was mainly rejected and hurt by people who I dearly loved or cared for dearly. Every relationship I would end up in left me hurt and bruised. I thought perhaps if I was good, kind and made sure to make the other person happy, they would love and care for me, but that didn't happen. I would give myself, my time, my energy, and my love to people, and in return, those people would want nothing to do with me. They would hurt me by embarrassing and emotionally draining my soul until there was nothing left. You get to a point where you are constantly checking yourself, what mistakes you have made to make that person do that to you. I used to blame myself for two things: firstly, for not being enough for that person, secondly, I would get angry at myself for not being enough for me, because I realized I was with those people because of the fear of being alone. The more love and care

I gave, the more rejection I got. I used to cry and cry for the countless attempts that I would give out my care, which would return in hurt, pain and rejection. Rejection is painful, being rejected feels like the world is discarding you. You feel alone and depressed at the fact that you don't hold any special place in anyone's heart. I would tell myself that I do not matter to anyone. There would be times where my phone would be quiet, no text, no calls, nothing. No matter how much I reached out, it would stay the same. I did not fit in with any group or demographic. When I found people who were willing to discuss those topics and have those dialogues, it was all older people, people who had jobs. These people would be people who would want to go for breakfast and dinners. At this point I am in university and barely making it because every penny I have, I have to put back into my business. My peers laugh at me for even considering starting and running a business. They laugh because I am always broke. The older ones who did have those conversations also can't see themselves in circles with a small 21-year-old girl. It was very difficult and painful because I didn't belong. I had to understand that neither myself or the people that rejected me were to blame for the pain and suffering I got from rejection. The rejection was just a vehicle for certain lessons that I had to learn from rejection, namely:

- The importance of self-love and acceptance.
- Because no one was willing to love and appreciate me, I made a choice to love and appreciate myself.

Sometimes you learn how to love yourself when no one else loves you. It is difficult, but you deserve your love more than anyone else's love. Your love for yourself should be independent of people and what they think of you. I had to learn that the hard way. Accepting yourself the way you are, even if no one else is willing to accept you.

- You learn to listen to yourself. If you were in the crowds with the masses you were not necessarily going to understand how to listen to yourself, but when you are alone, you find what voice you are bringing to the world. Yes, it takes time to understand how and why these things are happening to you, but you need to be strong. I found my voice, I know how my voice sounds and what impact I want to make with my voice.

- As you are listening to yourself you develop a sense of self-knowledge. It is when spending time with yourself that you discover those secrets. I say they are secrets because only those who have gone through self-discovery can fully say they know themselves. I am not saying that people who have a lot of friends and love from society don't love or know themselves, but I am saying that those who didn't receive that love have more agency to discover things about themselves more than having others find out those things about them. Imagine not having anyone love you to the extent of which you want them to, now imagine having to derive that love from within your-self. Imagine having to fill yourself with that love in order to find validation within yourself. The thing that I had to learn from the benefits of rejection is that I AM ENOUGH.

- You are enough, you are enough for yourself, your voice is enough, the way you look is enough, your kindness is enough, your care is enough, it is all enough for you. As you find out more about your-self, you find out that what you enjoy is enough, what makes you happy is enough, not for anyone else, but yourself. You are enough.

Cry, cry and cry more because it hurts, but it is also important that you find the strength to look at yourself and say, "I AM ENOUGH." It is going to be difficult at first, but I have realized that sometimes we lose people in order to learn how to be independent without people. Learning to be independent takes a lot of strength because having people to depend on is much easier, but if you find yourself in the position where you receive rejection then know that you will come out stronger and much better than you were. You will be braver in your decision making because you trust the voice inside that you discovered in the absence of people. Don't fear loneliness, when you have yourself you won't be lonely. You will be comfortable with your presence. Trust in the power of your existence regardless of people. Loneliness is a mental state, you are not lonely when you have yourself.

I had to understand that I will meet people, but I am happy with or without people because people do not define me or my state of happiness. A mistake that many people make is that in that phase of separation from the world they despair, and it is normal to, but you have to pull yourself up and out again. Rather spend more time investing in yourself, you deserve that. Do not allow people to determine your happiness and sometimes we find ourselves in those positions because we have centered people as the epitome of our happiness. Let us engage in the true sense of happiness, which is happiness that cannot be dismayed or put down. This kind of happiness makes you happy regardless of if people love you or not. At this point I am grateful to everyone who has rejected me, hurt me and caused me pain. It is now that I realize that it is okay, it is okay to be enough for myself. Be careful who you allow inside your heart, because we always get hurt when we allow everyone and everything that comes our way into our hearts. We need to be careful not to do that. Once you allow that loneliness to happen, that time of separation and segregation from the world to deal with yourself, allow that time to introspect in order to know what you want for yourself. Don't allow anyone in the perimeters of your heart. Once you are patient enough, you will get the space to receive the people that have the same energy as you. I used to cry because I always met and had friends who would just hurt me until I realized I was the one who was hurt, and I had to let go of the hurt and be patient to meet people who wouldn't hurt me. I urge you to spend time with yourself. I know it's going to be hard at first, but you will make it. I had to realize that the reason why God is taking all these people away from me was because He wanted me to learn how to be comfortable in myself and in Him without the pleasure of friends.

DIARY ENTRY: 5 OCTOBER 2018

I am at the lowest point I have been in my life. I say these are the times where I am getting the taste of being grown up. I have always had a level of maturity, but certain things come along with growing up. I am becoming the woman that I have always wanted to be because I am facing challenges and obstacles that not just anyone gets. I am in a financial pit, owing over R60 000 debt. In my second semester I decided to move from a place I was staying at because I was not satisfied with the place, and also the rent was very expensive, and I wanted to save money so that I could invest it in my business. I moved out and unfortunately, I was bound by a contract, the contract making me liable for over R40 000 rent balance due. I have been transferred to credit collectors, meaning I receive an email and call almost every week reminding me to pay over R40 000. On top of that I am currently owing a friend over R3000 who loaned me to make my recent event a success. She is expecting her money and I do not have any at all. I also recently received an email from SARS for owing money in return, my biggest desire having been that my business doesn't require to deal with SARS issues and being on the good side of the law. Also, my business account is in over R1000 overdraft where I have received notification of making a payment to avoid closure of my business account. Being so disciplined and focused I had never thought that at the age of 20 I would find myself in such a financial hurdle, one that I cannot comprehend how I am going to get over. I cannot consider how I will go about paying for any of it. Being in second year and having the pressures of university and academia, being able to live my life on the minimum has made me realize the importance of sharing, giving, and trusting God to make a way where there seems to be no way. I have decided to place things into God's hands now. For this reason, I am going to start afresh. I will take time off for the next couple of months to re-evaluate things and begin 2019 on a different note. I will work hard and stay focused. I am so happy with the woman I am becoming. I thank God for the abounding strength He is showering me with, nothing can compare to it.

DIARY ENTRY: 11th FEBRUARY 2019

I am currently facing a time where I want to change courses, from theater to a film and media/ television degree. A decision that took me two years to finally make. And I don't know why I wasn't making the change, why I stayed with a degree that I know for sure I don't want to do. A part of me wanted to prove to myself and my family that I am not a quitter. I wanted to show them that because in the beginning I said I liked the course, only saying so because I had no other option because I didn't apply to any other university. I wanted to prove that I was going to finish this course that I knew for a fact that I was not going to be able to do or had no interest or enjoyment in. Whilst I was doing it, I felt like I was suffocating and that nothing was right. I felt lost and confused on campus. I slowly felt like I was losing a part of myself, like I was losing my sense of existence, the one feeling that makes me uncomfortable. I didn't know what I was doing, what my role was and how I fit in. Everything I did was wrong, it felt wrong, it was wrong for me. I made the decision at the end of second year that I can no longer continue. I cannot continue sabotaging myself and my sense of serenity. It was one of the most painful experiences ever because I was told I don't qualify for the course (film and media). I was told that the marks I had acquired from theater were not enough to change to a general BA. I felt a lump in my heart, like I have never felt before. I felt sad and confused, and because I had decided to take this journey on my own, I cried on my own. I prayed to God to hear my heart, to sympathize with my heart. It was devastating and painful. The only thing I knew was that I didn't want to go back to drama school. I knew that for me to be sane I needed to leave that environment and be where and do what my actual passion is, film and television. The first time I told my mom about this painful feeling I had for two years she told me about the embarrassing things people were going to say if I dropped out of varsity. And after explaining to her that I was not going to drop out, but merely change courses, she understood it as a failure, a disgrace and failed to listen to my reasoning. I had to do this for me and not for everyone else. I remember the reactions I received when people found out about this decision. I made the decision, so I had to be strong and go through it all.

CHAPTER 7

A SPACE FOR YOU

THERE ARE MANY OF US WHO FIND OURSELVES IN SPACES that bring havoc to our spirit, that unsettle us. These spaces make us uncomfortable, sad and depressed. We pressure ourselves in order to please other people and to avoid seeing ourselves as failures. We trap ourselves by continuing to engulf ourselves with surroundings that don't maximize our potential. At drama school I felt restricted, misunderstood, and judged. I felt like I didn't belong. After several accounts of introspection, I realized it was not anyone or anything that was the problem there, I was the problem. I didn't belong there, I was not meant to be there. I realized that we must run away from spaces where we don't belong, it's detrimental and harmful to the spirit to be in spaces where your energy is unwelcome and your sense of being is disallowed.

How Do You Know You Don't Belong in a Space?

You feel it! Something in the way things are done, you are constantly discomforted. You know you don't belong when the only reason why you are there is because it seems like there is no other option but to be there. For me it was just the energy of the space. My personality, and character was often judged and misinterpreted not because anyone was deliberately doing this but because I didn't belong. I was very unhappy and didn't find people I could resonate with. The ones I did spend time with, made me constantly doubt myself. I always knew from the very first day that I don't like being there, but I suck it up in order to not feel like a loser. I dreaded waking up in the morning and was constantly complaining about how I didn't want to be there, which made me come up with several explanations to myself as to why I should be there. The more I tried to convince myself the more I didn't want to be. What makes people in a space strive and work well together is when they allow each other's energies to co-exist in a space. I felt like I was displaced and that is how I knew I didn't belong in that space. There are several other spaces that I had left in order to save my spirit from harm. Not to say you won't get challenges in every space, but you should never settle for a space that doesn't allow you to be you!

How Do You Get Out of the Space?

Simply go! It might not be easy but just go. For me I did not tell anyone I was leaving, I just left. That eliminated other people's opinions which might make you reconsider getting out. For me the thought of leaving was constantly on my mind and as much as I tried to suppress it, the more it haunted me. The only thing left was for me to go. I would say the first step would be that you talk to yourself. Ask yourself why you are in that space. Sometimes we get ourselves in spaces we thought would be best for us, and when we find out that they are not what we thought, we stay because we are afraid of what people will say. I would say never seek people's approval or validation in order to do anything. I am not saying don't seek advice, mentorship and guidance, that is essential, however if your spirit doesn't agree with a space, run!

How Do You Find a Space for You?

You will feel it. It does not mean that the space will be all fabulous all around, you will find challenges in it too, but you will feel that you belong. You will feel at home; your spirit will rest, and you will be motivated to work harder and strive in that environment. The space will make you happy. When you don't feel awful in the morning about going to a place then you should know for sure that you are in the right space. The space will allow you to radiate and will bring the best out of you. The space will make you want to be the best. It will make you happy. The energies in the space will align with your energy and you will find yourself in full joy because you are where you are supposed to be.

CHAPTER 8

TOOLS FOR THE JOURNEY

I HAVE LEARNT SOMETHING THAT I BELIEVE EVERYONE should know and understand, you are here on this Earth to travel a journey with challenges that will take you to the next level. Like a game of Candy Crush, in order to go to level two, you need to overcome level one. There are two things that could happen in every level:

1. You could either be strategic, smart, and aware that you have started and there is no going back. You can overcome the tactics handed to you. Use points, rewards, or anything you have in order to overcome that stage. You can focus your attention and time on

making sure that you don't get distracted. You could push and push and push and push until you finally finish that stage.

2. You could get in that stage, get distracted and not go to the next stage. You could stay in that one stage, not because you are unable to go to the next level, but because you are not applying the fundamentals of completing a stage. You will then stay in that stage and after several attempts and failures to execute those, you start blaming those people and things that distracted you. You start hating yourself for the continuous failure and then you will be stuck and not move forward.

The fundamentals to completing and going past every stage are as follow:

a. KNOW THAT YOU ARE IN A JOURNEY.

The first and most important thing is being aware that you are on a journey and that the journey will have challenges. Be cognizant that the stage has challenges that are waiting for your hard work in order to be accomplished. Being aware means, you need to be ready for challenges and not fear them as they will come. So that when they do approach you, you are not afraid. Fear of being challenged means you are afraid of growth. Stand with your head held high and know that you will have those challenges and you will overcome them. Which is the first step to a winner's attitude. Part of being ready is being mentally prepared. What sets apart the winner from the rest in a marathon is that the winner understood that they are in a race and that they must win! What enables you this mentality is not paying attention to the excuses your circumstances give you. If you pay attention to those you won't be mentally prepared for the journey. The fact that you are aware of challenges, will eliminate fear and will mentally prepare you for the journey.

b.   PREPARE.

The first preparation is mental. The next important preparation is physical. You need to physically prepare every cell in your body to be able to tackle and take the journey. You need to do everything necessary to prepare your body, challenge your body and enable your body to take on the challenge. I say challenge because everything that you get faced with in your journey to success becomes a challenge and only the ones who conquered the challenges are the ones with the tag successful next to their names. Just like Candy Crush, it is your body that must duck and turn to avoid those obstacles. It is your body that will have sleepless nights, it is your body that will cry in fatigue. It is your body that will have to run around trying to make success a reality. You need to take care of your body because it is your tool to reaching your destination. You need to take care of your body and inside your body is your soul.

c.   TAKE CARE OF YOUR SOUL.

Many people focus on every other aspect and element of the success journey, forgetting the importance of the soul. The soul is a very essential part of our being. The order of being is as follows: Soul, Mind, Heart, and then Body (SMHD). This hierarchy exists in each one of us, and it is our responsibility to take care of this hierarchy. This means that we need to take care of the hegemonic soul first. It is highly essential to take care of your soul. The soul is in your body therefore if you are taking care of the body you need to also take care of the soul. You take care of your soul by nurturing it, and you nurture it by feeding it. It is your fed soul that will help give you strength. When you feel tired and weary, your soul boosts your mind and body to go forth. It is a soul unfed that breeds negative energy, and dwells in disappointments and failures. If your soul is fed, you know where to draw your strength from. Your soul will be challenged in many ways, therefore it needs to be strong. Constantly feed yourself with positive energy. Let your soul endure any spiritual and mental challenge presented to you. Surrounding yourself with negative energy will drain you and you will get distracted from your journey. If there aren't any people around, to instill that positive energy, then rather spend much of your time with yourself until you meet those people. Even if it means you will be lonely then so be it, but avoid toxicity from your space. Many people give up or get discouraged because they get infected by others' negative energy. Negative energy is dangerous for your soul because you lose the meaning of your sense of humanity. And by sense of humanity, I mean you lose yourself, you lose the ability to see the value of your own dreams. Negative energy takes away your passion, takes away your sense of identity. It is a force that requires a strong soul and spirituality to overcome. You need to stay away from that energy because it will waste a lot of your time. You don't need all that time wasted, you could be focusing all that time and energy on building yourself. Protect your soul. Taking care of your soul means understanding what makes your soul specifically different and unique and why your soul was placed in your specific body. Taking care of your soul is being aware of what it needs to feed on and then feeding it. Ensuring that you let in your soul what is necessary and what is necessary is its food. Feed your soul by meditation, prayer, and intimacy with God. Have at least one or two days a week where you sit down on your own, in a space with nothing else but yourself. Switch everything off, your TV, your laptop, your phone, make sure you are away from everyone. Spend this time to investigate your soul, find out where your soul is. Discover your soul, feed your soul. Feed yourself with positive and healthy energy. There are always going to be people who will constantly try and shift you and distract you from the discovery of your soul. Your soul needs continuous feeding of meditation. People are very broken, people are very hurt and their intention, unconsciously, is to bring upon the same to others. The most important thing is that you must become selfish about your soul, become selfish about you. No one and nothing should possess power over your soul, it is yours, therefore you must protect it. Guard the energies you bring into your space, guard the souls that surround your soul. Block out all negative energies that bring your soul discomfort.

d.   GROW:

A successful life is one filled with constant growth. Positive energy and attitude will motivate you to want to grow. People who are not willing to accept growth become stagnant. You become stagnant when you are unwilling to accept change, difference, and growth. What about growth is important you ask? Well in order to grow, first you need to understand that you don't know everything and in that way your spirit will be willing to accept lessons given to you. Then you must open yourself to challenges. You are the one who should make the decision, therefore no one can force you. You must open yourself up and take any opportunity to grow yourself whether it seems small or big. Most people reject and look down on small opportunities to grow. Any and every opportunity that you receive you should be willing and able to grow yourself.

e.   WORK HARD

Work hard and stay focused on that work. It is easy to get distracted and unmotivated from working hard. Working hard is tiring and draining but it is worth it. The unfortunate part of hard work is that sometimes no one sees it. It is not glamorous, instead it's gloomy and often directionless. Most times you know the destination, you know what you want to achieve but it is difficult figuring out how you are going to do it. There is no clear direction and manual of steps to take in order to get to the end. It is very unfortunate that no one wants to put in the hard work but want the glorious victorious end. The process is the most important part of the journey. Trust the process, enjoy the process, find those valuable lessons and challenges in the process.

f.   PERSEVERE

Never ever give up. Perseverance is an attribute that requires a very strong minded and willed person. I learnt this principle when I used to watch my grandmother rebuild a shack that had burnt from the Fires of Joe-Slovo. She understood that if she did not rebuild that shack then we wouldn't have a roof over our heads. So no matter how many times the shack would burn to the ground, she would rebuild it. I am happy that I learnt this principle from my grandmother, otherwise I would have not been able to have a thick backbone that refuses to let go of her dreams because of challenges. Just like my grandmother, I understand that if I don't pursue what I need to, then I am preventing my sense of being from manifesting. My ambitions and dreams need a shelter and no matter how many times I fall due to disappointments, I must pick myself up and try again. Fall, get up, fall again, fall again, get up again. Do it until you are convinced that you are very well equipped at it. Like driving, you need to do it consistently until it becomes second nature to you. Where you get to a point where you are so good at it that nothing that anyone can do can take your ability to do it away.

REMEMBER...............

Above all, I would like to remind you that you are worthy, you are beautiful, you are enough! You are talented and you are gifted. You are important, you are loved, you are amazing. You are kind and gentle. You are genuine, you are real, you are true. You are bright, you are happy, you are the light. You are brave, you are powerful, you are incredible. You are smart, you are ambitious, you are the world's greatest. You have ideas, visions and goals that are going to change the world. You are in God's image, you are a god. Trust yourself, love yourself, embrace yourself. Be happy. Find peace inside your heart and never ever allow anyone to take that away from you. Laugh, love and be happy. Your purpose is waiting for you, the world is waiting for you to manifest your purpose.

Wishing you strength, love and light,
Vuyo Joboda

About the Author

Born and raised in Kwalanga, Cape Town South Africa Vuyo is a bright, beautiful, and empowered young woman, and an aspiring media mogul working hard in changing the landscape of media in the African continent. As the Founder of the Vuyo Joboda Network, Young Bold Black Global Leadership Collective, and VN Streaming, Vuyo has cemented her role as one of the youngest executive producers and directors on the continent. Her goal, through her tech-startup company and her continuous efforts in the industry, is to create innovative solutions that integrate technology into media and tailor-making those to be best suitable for Africa in a global fashion.

The eloquent TV host is known for her talk show expertise as the host of "Going Global with Vuyo Joboda' where she has conversations with global guests sharing information that affects us all. She is a final year UCT Film and Media student and a prolific researcher of the industry. Vuyo is also a well renowned internationally trained and recognized speaker and MC whose global presence is evidently growing as she has shared stages with Hollywood executives David Prescott, an Academy Award-winning Director and Producer, Peter A Ramsey, and Aaron Warner.

In 2017, at the age of 19, she took to the TEDx stage, ending her talk with a standing ovation, and has been part of the TEDx Cape Town organization. She has graced the stage as an MC and facilitator amongst other roles. Another hat that Vuyo effortlessly wears is the "Event organizer", and this year marks her 8th year in this role. She has organized numerous events including the International Fabulous Woman Gala Dinner, the annual Young Bold Black Awards, VN Global Media and Entertainment Awards, and more.

South Africa's President Mr. Cryil Ramaphosa has acknowledged her contribution to the African literature industry for her book, 21. Vuyo is a force to be reckoned with and a rising global brand and is shining her light brightly.

Connect with the Author

Connect with me on social media:
Instagram: @VuyoJoboda
Facebook: @VuyoJoboda
Twitter: @VJoboda

YOUR WORDS HAVE POWER

For the next 21 days I encourage you to write your innermost thoughts in discovery of power.

Day 1

Day 2

Day 3

Day 4

Day 5

Day 6

Day 7

Day 8

Day 9

Day 10

Day 11

Day 12

Day 13

Day 14

Day 15

Day 16

Day 17

Day 18

Day 19

Day 20

Day 21

NEVER FORGET YOU ARE THE LIGHT.